Sam and Pa

d You Ca

We Can Help Our Mom

by Amanda Litz

illustrated by
Cynthia Garcia

Traveler's Trunk Publishing
Cedar Springs, Michigan

To Jacob, Sierra, Mason, and Ethan –
you are my inspiration.
– A.L.

ISBN 978-0-9841496-1-2

CPSIA facility code: BP 313627

www.travelerstrunkpublishing.com

Printed in the United States of America

I am Sam.

I am Pam.

We are twins.

But we do not
look the same.

I am tall.
I am small.

My hair is short
and black.

My hair is long
and red.

This is our mom.

She works at home.

We can help our mom.

Our room is a mess.

I can make my bed.

I can pick up my toys.

The dog needs
to go for a walk.

I can walk the dog.

I see the mailman.

I can get the mail.

The trash is full.

I can take out the trash.

Dinner is ready.

I can set the table.

It is time to
do the dishes.

I can fill the sink
with water.

We can wash the dishes.

Now the work is done.

Mom said we
did a good job.

We like to help our mom.

Can you help your mom?

What can you do?

Sam and Pam
are proud of
you!